This book belongs to

....

Address ....

....

....

Age ....

Written by Brian Miles,
Illustrated by Ken McKie.

Published by
Grandreams Limited,
Jadwin House, 205/211 Kentish Town Road, London NW5 2JU.

Printed in Czechoslovakia.

ISBN 0 86227 899 6

KM42

Teddy Tales in this book

TEDDY
on
Christmas Day

Teddy opened one eye, then the other,
"Don't rise too early," had said his mother.
He lifted his head and looked around,
What was that parcel in ribbons bound?

Silently he rose and crept across the floor,
     Gazing at the parcel by his bedroom door.
It was beautifully wrapped with ribbons and bows,
     Teddy tingled with joy from his head to his toes!

Could it be the present,
    That he'd waited for so long?
Trembling he unwrapped it,
    Hoping he would not be wrong.

Teddy

Off came the coloured ribbons,
Off came the pretty bows,
Off came the wrapping paper,
Teddy whispered "Here goes.

With legs astride and beaming smile,
  He strummed a shattering chord,
Pretending he was a pop-star,
  He said, "Here's my new record."
It's Christmas today, Christmas today,
  Oh what fun is Christmas day.
Presents to open, goodies to eat,
  Christmas day is one big treat.'"

"Teddy dear!" his mother called,
"That was very nice, I'm sure.
But please go back to bed now,
It's only twenty past four."

Teddy lovingly stroked his new guitar,
And climbed back into bed.
He tried closing his eyes but could not sleep,
As music filled his head.

Soon the first rays of sunshine,
       Began to herald Christmas day.
Teddy sprang up out of bed,
       And his guitar began to play!
He just could not wait to show his friends,
       How lucky he had been,
He thought he was the luckiest bear,
       The world had ever seen!

Teddy thanked his mummy and daddy,
    For his lovely new guitar.
Then sat down to eat porridge and cream,
    And some honey from the jar.

He had arranged to meet the other bears,
Around about half past ten.
So with guitar slung over his shoulder,
Set off for their woodland den.

Arriving at the woodland den,
Teddy had a big surprise.
When he opened the wooden door,
He could scarce believe his eyes.

Jimbo began with a roll on the drums,
He was wearing a nice green coat.
Bessy blew loud on a big slide trombone,
And Belle's trumpet hit a high note.

They had all received musical instruments,
    On this lovely Christmas day.
And now with Teddy playing on his new guitar,
    They began to play away.

Soon the whole woodland den was rocking,
Rocking to the foot-tapping beat.
The beat of the Teddy Bear Jazz Band,
What a wonderful Christmas treat!

"It's time to go," said Teddy at last,
    "But come to my house tonight.
Bring your folks and we'll have a good time,
    I'm sure it will be alright."

Teddy's mummy and daddy beamed their delight,
As they greeted them one and all.
They prepared lots of food, rolled back the carpet,
And said, "Come on let's have a ball!"

All the bears had now arrived,
And the party was really swinging.
Lionel Bear, who had a lovely voice,
Led them with his singing.

Then Teddy stood up and raised his glass,
"I propose a little toast,
To all you wonderful friends of mine,
To the bears I love the most."

The Teddy Bear Jazz Band played all night,
And they all had a wonderful time.
They clinked their glasses in a Christmas toast,
And then all together sang Auld Lang Syne.

Outside the snow began to fall,
    Soft and cold and glittering white.
And in the sky a bright star shone,
    On this magical Christmas night.

TEDDY
and
A Christmas Visit

Snow was falling on the woodland pines,
And the bears were in their den.
"You know, I've been thinking," Teddy said,
"It's time we called on old Ben."

"It will be Christmas day tomorrow,
    And I know you will all agree,
Let's take some presents to dear old Ben,
    And help to decorate his tree."

"That's a splendid idea," Jimbo said,
"Let's get started straightaway.
We will see how many nice presents,
We can pile up on our sleigh."

And so off into the forest,
  Went the intrepid little bears.
Pushing and pulling their sleigh along,
  Through the woodland that was theirs.

Soon they began to collect things,
From their friends along the way.
The squirrels gave them hazelnuts,
Put by for a special day.

The bees said, "Here's some honeycomb,
With Christmas greetings to dear Ben.
We often visit his garden,
In fact, it's time we went again."

The rabbits gave them some orange pippins,
Preserved in their underground store.
And Grandma Bear gave a beautiful cake,
As they passed by her cottage door.

Toad of Toad Hall gave some nice Christmas crackers,
With a card which began "My Dear Ben..."
Whilst Rat and Mole gave a long-playing record,
Of the great Des O'Connor's Top Ten!

Miss Bunty Bear had knitted some socks,
    "For my very sweet and dear Ben.
I'm not sure what his size is," she blushed,
    "So I've knitted him a large ten."

Lionel Bear gave some damson wine,
    "To be consumed in moderation."
Whilst Lionel's mum gave some fairy cakes,
    "Suitable for any occasion."

They picked some mistletoe and holly,
 And decorated Bessy's hat.
Belle decorated hers with snowdrops,
 Saying, "What do you think of that?"

Teddy found some fresh wild mushrooms,
And some rosemary and thyme.
Then coming to old Ben's cottage,
Heard him sing a little rhyme.

"Oh lack-a-day, Oh lack-a-day,
How sweet does my garden grow.
If only I could see my friends,
Much happiness would I know."

"Here we are! Here we are!"
        Came a loud chorus from the Bears.
"Forget your worries and your woes,
        Your troubles and your cares."

With that they knocked on the great oak door,
Which Ben opened with a smile.
"How nice to see you," said old Ben,
"I think of you all the while."

The bears gave Ben all the gifts they had brought,
  He was delighted as can be.
"You're just in time for a freshly baked cake,
  And a nice pot of Earl Grey tea."

They decorated the Christmas tree,
With tinsel and coloured balls.
Then hung mistletoe, holly and ivy,
All around the cottage walls.
Very soon then old Ben's cottage,
Was looking festive as can be.
A roaring log fire in the grate,
And a beautiful Christmas tree.

Ben was so happy,
    That the bears had come to call,
And though he liked the presents,
    Seeing them was best of all.
And so as dusk began to fall,
    The bears said their fond farewells,
They turned and waved and headed home,
    To the sound of Christmas bells.

Content that they had brought some cheer,
    To a good and kindly bear,
They reminded each other that,
    Christmas was a time for care.

The creatures of the forest,
Are silent as they lay.
Knowing that tomorrow,
Is a very special day.
And so this little story ends,
Of creatures all of whom are friends,
Who in the forest silence lay,
Await the dawn of Christmas day.

TEDDY
and The Snowman

"Hold on tightly!" said Teddy,
"here we jolly well go!"
The four-bear toboggan,
Went hurtling over the snow.

Down the hill they roared,
    At tremendous speed.
Jimbo at the back,
    Teddy in the lead!

Up and over humps and hillocks,
     Flashing through the trees.
Speeding over the crisp white snow,
     What a super wheeze!

Down into the village square,
Then past the Christmas tree.
Through the high street, round the bend,
To Teddy's house for tea!

Mrs Bear had baked a chocolate cake,
There were toasted muffins too.
Said Teddy, "After we have finished tea,
I know just what we can do."

"We'll make a snowman six feet high,
with a hat and a pipe and tie.
And we'll raise money for Old Age Bears,
from everyone passing by."

"We'll give them a Christmas party,
    the best they have ever had.
With Christmas cake and hot mince pies,
    for every Gran and Grandad."

"So come on then everybody,
    let's make our snowman grow."
Then off they trooped to the village green,
    To make a man of snow.

Teddy and Belle rolled some snow,
Into a great round ball.

Then they piled more snow on top,
To make him very tall.

Bessy and Jimbo made his head,
And gave him two big eyes.
Then a mouth and a bright red nose,
And two big ears besides!

They gave him a pipe and a nice bow tie,
And then a black top hat.
Stones for his buttons and a walking stick,
And then a final pat.

Said Teddy, "Christmas is next Tuesday,
we must start collecting now.
Shake your buckets and rattle your tins,
and let's really show them how!"

Lots of their friends had gathered around,
Eager to give a hand.
The Christmas Spirit had come to life,
Thanks to this merry band!

"O Come All Ye Faithful",
        Sang the village choir.
Whilst chestnuts were roasting,
        On a glowing fire.

Skaters waltzed hand-in-hand,
    On the village pond frozen hard.
Snowflakes fell all around,
    Like a beautiful Christmas card.

The village bears gave generously,
    And soon the buckets were full.
"We've got more than enough," Teddy said,
    "to give a party for all."

So on Christmas Eve they assembled,
      In the village hall as planned.
All the young bears dressed up as waiters,
      And everything was grand!
There were hot mince pies and Christmas cake,
      And lots of crackers and pop.
Everyone had a lovely time,
      And wished it would never stop.

The bears had a splendid party,
     "Thanks to Teddy," they said.
"Very soon it will be midnight,
     and we must go to bed.
For it's Christmas Eve and Santa's coming,
     with presents for all good young bears."
So they said, "Good night," and went to their beds,
     In rooms at the top of the stairs.

But as the village clock chimed twelve,
The snowman stood in his place.
A merry twinkle in his eye,
And a smile upon his face.

TEDDY
and
Santa`s Sleigh Ride

It was Christmas Eve in the forest,
And the snow lay crisp and deep.
Stars glittered bright from a moonlit sky,
And everyone lay asleep.

All except Teddy that was,
    Who gazed through a frosted pane.
At pine-clad snow covered hills,
    Thinking it's Christmas again.

Suddenly, coming over the tree-tops,
He saw a wondrous sight.
It was Santa Claus Bear and his reindeer,
Flying through the still night.

Teddy gasped in wonder,
    And jumped up from his bed.
He ran to the window,
    To look at Santa's sled.
The reindeer stopped outside Teddy's house,
    Breath on the night air froze.
Santa sat on a big pile of sacks,
    Rubbing his big red nose.

"Ho! Ho!" he chortled, looking up,
     "you should be fast asleep.
If you don't go straight back to bed,
     your presents I must keep."

"I'm sorry," said Teddy,
        "but I cannot sleep.
Santa, can I come with you?
        You've lots of presents to deliver tonight,
is there nothing I can do?"

Santa laughed and said, "Come on down!
    Climb up here upon my sleigh.
There's lots of work to do this night,
    we must quickly be away."

The reindeer snorted and stamped their hooves,
    And then with the speed of light,
Soaring high above the snow-white trees,
    They sped off into the night.

Around the world they travelled,
   Leaving presents everywhere.
Then back to Greenland to load again,
   With presents for every bear.

They went down to Australia,
   With gifts for Koala bear.

Then on to far off China,
   For the Panda bears so rare.

p they flew to the Arctic,
    With gifts for the Polar bear.

Then to North America,
    For the Grizzlys that are there.

They filled up socks and stockings,
    With nuts and oranges and things.
And hopped from chimney to chimney,
    Just as if they both had wings.

On they flew with bells a-jingling,
  Bells jingling all the way.
Across the roofs of sleeping towns,
  Went Santa's Christmas sleigh.

They tiptoed into bedrooms,
    And read letters pinned to doors.
Then silently left presents,
    On carpeted bedroom floors.

They stopped high on top of a mountain,
Just for a quick tasty snack,
Of Christmas Pudding and hot mince pies,
That Santa took from his sack.

They dashed across the roof of St Pauls,
On their way to Timbuktu.

Onto the White House in Washington,

Over Sydney Harbour too!

They flew up the side of Mount Everest,
On their way to Katmandu.
Then down to Ashdown Forest in Sussex,
With gifts for Winnie The Pooh!

Then Santa turned to Teddy,
    "This evening's work is done," he said.
"I must go back to Greenland,
    when you're safely tucked up in bed."

Teddy woke early the next morning,
    Had it all just been a dream?
Had he really raced around the world,
    With Santa Claus' reindeer team?
He looked with wonder at his presents,
    Heaped on his bedroom floor.
Then at a note that he could see pinned,
    Onto his bedroom door!

"Thank you Teddy," said the note,
"you deserve my full applause.
A Merry Christmas to you,
with much love from Santa Claus!"